Carla's Sandwich

Written by Debbie Herman   Illustrated by Sheila Bailey

Flashlight Press

New York

For my mom, with love.
Thanks for always leaving out the onions. –DH

To my Auntie Sigrid, who always made the best cardamom bread
and goat cheese sandwiches in the world. –SB

Special thanks to Becker, Fabio, and The Investors.
And in appreciation of the support of the Posse! –DH

Copyright © 2004 by Flashlight Press
Text copyright © 2004 by Debbie Herman
Illustrations copyright © 2004 by Sheila Bailey

First Edition – September 2004

Library of Congress Control Number: 2004104836

ISBN 0-972-92252-0

Editor: Shari Dash Greenspan
Graphic Design: The Virtual Paintbrush
This book was typeset in Skia.
Illustrations were rendered using a combination of watercolor and digital media.

Distributed by Independent Publishers Group

Flashlight Press • 527 Empire Blvd • Brooklyn, NY 11225
www.FlashlightPress.com

Carla brought weird sandwiches to school. Buster noticed it first.
He was sitting next to Carla at lunch one Monday.
"EEEW! What are you eating?" Buster asked. "It's all green and slimy!"
"It's an olive, pickle and green bean sandwich," said Carla. "I made it myself.
Would you like some? I brought extra."
"No way!" said Buster, pinching his nose. "That's gross!"
"It's not gross," said Carla. "It's different. I like to be different."
"It's not different," said Buster. "It's gross." And he went to sit next to Leslie instead.

On Tuesday Carla's sandwich was long
with something yellow and white oozing out at the sides.
"What in the world is that?" asked Leslie.
"It's my Banana-Cottage-Cheese Delight," said Carla, "on a tasty toasted baguette."

"Bananas and cottage cheese?" asked Leslie, sticking out her tongue. "That's disgusting."

"It's not disgusting," said Carla. "It's creative."

"It's disgusting," said Leslie, and she went to sit next to Natie instead.

On Wednesday Carla's sandwich was orange and brown and lumpy.
It crunched when she bit into it.
"Ugh!" said Natie, who was sitting next to her now. "What is that?"
"I call it Carla's Crunch," said Carla. "It's peanut butter, crackers and cheddar cheese
in a lovely pita bread. I brought extra. Would you like some?"

"No way!" said Natie, scrunching his face. "That's sick!"
"It's not sick," said Carla. "It's unique."
"It's sick," said Natie. And he went to sit next to Marcus instead.

On Thursday Carla brought a chopped liver, potato chip and cucumber sandwich.

On Friday she brought a sardine and mustard sandwich with sunflower seeds.

By Monday, no one wanted to sit next to Carla, so she ate by herself.

At the end of the day, Miss Pimento made an announcement.
"Tomorrow we will have a picnic."
"Hurray!" everyone shouted. "A picnic! Yippee!"

The next day, when the lunch bell rang, the kids ran to get their picnic lunches.
"I have peanut butter and jelly," Natie announced to the class.
"I have baloney," said Leslie.
"Tuna," called Buster. "Hey Carla, what do you have?"

Carla didn't answer.
"It's probably a ketchup, spinach and jelly bean sandwich," joked Buster.
He and Leslie howled. So did Natie.
"It is not!" said Carla.

"Let's have some quiet in here," said Miss Pimento, "or we won't be able to have our picnic."
The class was suddenly silent.

Then the children followed Miss Pimento, two by two, down the hall,
out the door and down the block to the park.

"All right, everyone," said Miss Pimento. "Find a place to sit and bon appétit!"

Carla took a bite of her sandwich.
"Yuck!" said Buster, pointing at Carla's lunch. "What is that — a worm sandwich?"

"For your information," said Carla, "it's a lettuce, tomato, raisin, bean sprout, pretzel and mayonnaise sandwich. I call it the Combo Deluxe."

"It looks more like a **Wormbo** Deluxe!" teased Buster.

Leslie and Natie burst out laughing.

Buster rummaged through his knapsack. "Uh oh," he said quietly.
He rummaged some more. "Uh oh," he said again.
He dumped everything out of his bag.
"I can't believe it," Buster said sadly. "I forgot my sandwich."
"That's awful," said Leslie, biting into her baloney sandwich.
"A real bummer," said Natie, chomping on his peanut butter and jelly.

Soon everyone was eating – everyone except Buster.
Carla looked at Buster. She looked at her sandwich. She looked back at Buster.
"You can have one of mine," she offered. "I brought extra."
Some kids snickered.
"No thanks," said Buster glumly. "I'm not that desperate."

Doris ate her egg salad sandwich and Rufus ate his tuna.
Herbert ate his salmon salad sandwich and Barbara ate her turkey.
Buster's mouth began to water.
Buster looked at Carla's sandwich. "Maybe bean sprouts aren't so bad," he thought.
"It's really quite delicious," said Carla, catching Buster's glance.
Buster quickly turned away.

Susan ate her corned beef sandwich and Harris munched his taco.
Fabio ate his chicken sandwich and Gordon ate his meatloaf.
Buster was growing hungrier by the minute and his stomach growled loudly.
"Raisins are kind of fun," he thought, "and who doesn't like pretzels?"

Marcus ate his cheese sandwich and Darcy ate her bagel.
Buster eyed Carla's sandwich again.
"You don't know what you're missing..." Carla sang out.

Buster couldn't take it anymore. He looked around.
Everyone was busy eating.
No one was watching him.

"Okay," he whispered to Carla.
"Okay, what?" asked Carla.
"Okay, can I have one?" he whispered again.
"Can you have one what?" asked Carla.
Buster blurted impatiently, "Can I please have one of your sandwiches?"
Everyone looked up.

Carla smiled and handed Buster a Combo Deluxe.
Buster examined the lettuce, tomato, raisin, bean sprout,
pretzel and mayonnaise sandwich carefully.
He looked at Leslie, then Natie, then Carla.

And then he took a very small bite.

All eyes were watching as he chewed and swallowed.
"Well?" asked Leslie impatiently.
"Well?" asked Natie.
Buster didn't say anything.
He looked at everyone and took another bite.
And another. And another.

"I can't believe he's eating it!" said Natie in disgust.
"What does it taste like, Buster?" asked Leslie. "Is it gross?"

Buster didn't answer.
He was too busy eating.

When the last bite was gone, Buster licked his fingers and smacked his lips.
"Yum!" he said. "That was the best sandwich I ever ate!"
"It was?" asked Natie in horror.
"It was?" asked Leslie in dismay.
"It was!" said Buster, smiling at Carla.
Carla beamed.

"I bet you'd all enjoy the Combo Deluxe," said Carla. "Who'd like to try some?"

Slowly, Leslie raised her hand. Then Natie raised his.
Then Darcy, Susan, Rufus and Fabio.
Soon all the kids had their hands in the air.
Carla took her last sandwich, broke it into small pieces
and handed them out to everyone.

"Wow!" said Leslie, tasting her piece. "This is terrific!"

"Yeah!" said Natie. "It tastes great!"

"Tomorrow I'm going to bring a creative sandwich too," said Leslie. "Maybe it'll be a mustard sandwich with baked beans and French fries. What do you think of that, Carla?"

"Sounds good," said Carla. "And it's definitely creative."

"I'll bring a spaghetti and soy sauce sandwich," said Buster as he sat down next to Carla.

"Yum," said Carla and Leslie together.

"I don't know what I'm bringing yet," said Natie, "but it'll be unique."

The next day everyone in Miss Pimento's class brought an unusual sandwich to school.
There was an asparagus and salad dressing sandwich,
a pistachio and tangerine sandwich, and even a pizza sandwich.

"What did you bring today, Carla?" asked Buster.
"I'm not telling," said Carla. "You'll have to wait until lunch time."

The morning seemed to last forever, but finally the lunch bell rang.

While Buster was munching away on his spaghetti and soy sauce sandwich, he glanced over at Carla.

This time her sandwich was not green.
It was not slimy or lumpy
and nothing was oozing out at the sides.

"So, what kind of sandwich is that?" Buster asked.
"Yeah, Carla," said Leslie. "What's inside?"
Natie looked at Carla, waiting for an answer.

"Well," said Carla. "Today I have......peanut butter and jelly."
"Peanut butter and jelly?" asked Buster in disbelief.
"Peanut butter and jelly?" Leslie and Natie asked together.

"Peanut butter and jelly," said Carla, biting into her sandwich.
"I like to be different."